T0197410

Order this book online at www.trafford.com
or email orders@trafford.com

Most Trafford titles are also available at major online book retailers.

 www.trafford.com

North America & international
toll-free: 844 688 6899 (USA & Canada)
fax: 812 355 4082

Our mission is to efficiently provide the world's finest, most comprehensive book publishing
service, enabling every author to experience success. To find out how to publish your book,
your way, and have it available worldwide, visit us online at www.trafford.com

ISBN: 978-1-6987-0362-6 (sc)
ISBN: 978-1-6987-0365-7 (e)

Library of Congress Control Number: 2021909604

Print information available on the last page.

Trafford rev. 05/11/2021

The adventures of

Spotty
and
Sunny.

Book 4: A Fun Learning Series for kids

Time to party in the Everglades

Author/Pharmacist

SAISNATH BAIJOO

Jordi yawns lazily. He stretches his hands, He says. "You know Mommy. I am very tired. I was in school all day. Goodnight. I love you."

Mom smiles, "Goodnight, my love. Sweet dreams and say your prayers."

Jordi yawns again, "Mom, my brothers, Davin and Dominic talk a lot about Spotty and Sunny all day. Can you take me to the Everglades to meet them?"

Mom smiles and pinches his chubby cheeks, "Yes, sure but little boys need their sleep to grow strong like your dad."

Mom leaves his room and dims the light. Jordi is so tired after going to school all day in school. He starts dreaming.

"Can we take a ride on your magic carpet?" Miss. Can says.

Jordi smiles, "Yes sure."

Miss Can and Mr. Owl sits on Jordi's magic carpet and says, "Are you going to Spotty's birthday party?"

Jordi is happy. "Fairy Godmother, are we going to a party for Spotty? I love parties. It is fun. I like to dance and sing."

Fairy Godmother smiles, "Yes, son. Parties for kids are fun. Hold on. We are at Spotty's party."

As they reach Spotty's party, everyone is happy and claps.

Mrs. Owl hoots, "Who. Who! First, we placed red, blue, and white balloons in one big circle. Then, inside the big circle, there are smaller yellow, green, and pink balloons in the shape of a triangle. Then, there are black, white, and blue balloons in a square inside the circle. It is very nice."

Miss Can flaps her big white wings and boasts. "Aww thanks, but Mr. Owl and Mrs. Owl helped."

Mrs. Owl turns her head. "First, we made many shapes like squares, triangles, rectangle and circles."

Fairy Godmother interrupts the talkative Mrs. Owl. She waves her wand. "Jordi, you need nice party clothes and a birthday gift for Spotty. Today, everyone can live in the land and water."

"Yes," says Jordi, "Everyone is different, but we are all the same."

Everyone claps as Ms. Snapper, Sunny and
parents rises above the clear waters,

Jordi rushes to hug Spotty and Sunny. "Happy birthday, Spotty."

Spotty lifts Jordi on his head. He takes a selfie.

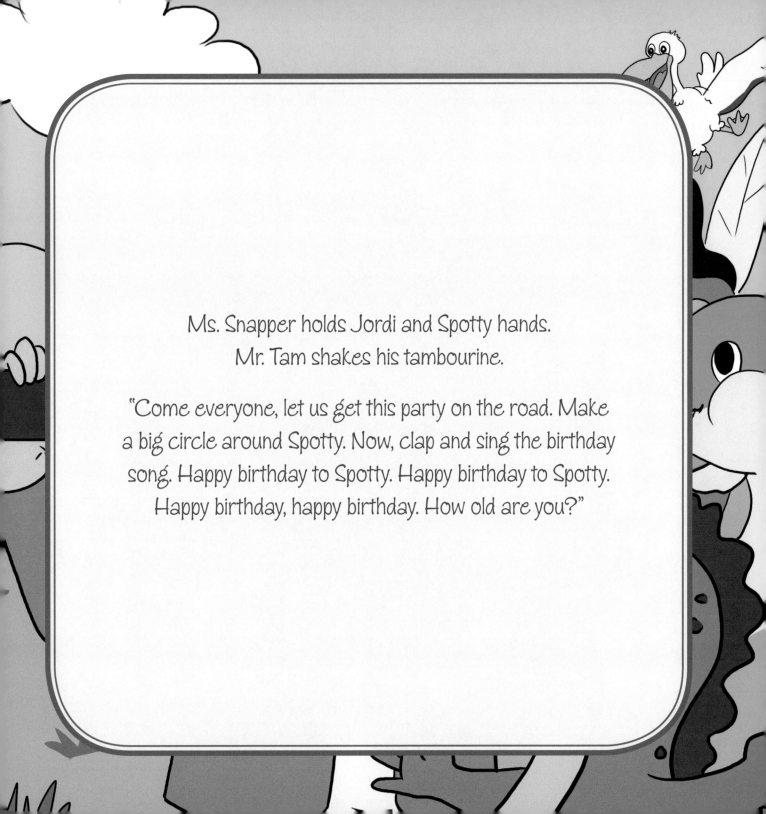

Ms. Snapper holds Jordi and Spotty hands.
Mr. Tam shakes his tambourine.

"Come everyone, let us get this party on the road. Make
a big circle around Spotty. Now, clap and sing the birthday
song. Happy birthday to Spotty. Happy birthday to Spotty.
Happy birthday, happy birthday. How old are you?"

Miss. Snapper waves her colorful fins and sings with Jordi, "Come and sing and do the Everglades dance. It is so easy. Now, move to the left and wave your left hand. Then, move to the right and wave your right hand. Now, one step forward and wave your hands and scream. We love you, Spotty. Clap your hand. Stand next to your friend to the left and go around in a circle. Round and round.

Jordi smiles and says, "I will now sing a special song for the birthday boy."

Mr. Tam plays his tambourine. Miss. Peacock spreads her colorful feathers and Miss Crabby hums.

Jordi sings and dances, "The more, we are together, together, the happier we will be. So, your friend is my friend, and everyone is your friend. We are different but everyone are friends." Everyone claps and dances through the night.

Jordi yawns to Fairy Godmother. "It was sure fun, but I am very tired. I was in school all day. I want to go home. We must come again." Fairy Godmother smiles, "Yes, my child. Your adventure has only started." Jordi hugs his Fairy Godmother. "Thank you for a wonderful time."

In the morning, Jordi awakes with a party hat on his head.

Jordi is asleep with his party hat. His parents come in his room.

Mom says, "Now, where did my baby get this party hat?"

Was Jordi dreaming?

Thank you for your order on sbaijoo.com
Text me at (786) 223-2563
Follow me on Facebook, Instagram, and Twitter

Printed in the United States
by Baker & Taylor Publisher Services